INTERLOPER

W0081941

INTERLOPER

Poems

L. S. Klatt

University of Massachusetts Press

AMHERST

Copyright © 2009 by L. S. Klatt
All rights reserved
Printed in the United States of America

LC 2009005895
ISBN 978-1-55849-697-2

Designed by Sally Nichols
Set in ITC Mona Lisa and Granjon
Printed and bound by BookMobile, Inc.

Library of Congress Cataloging-in-Publication Data

Klatt, L. S.
Interloper : poems / L.S. Klatt.
p. cm.
"Winner of the 2008 Juniper Prize for Poetry."
ISBN 978-1-55849-697-2 (pbk. : alk. paper)
I. Title.
PS3611.L39I67 2009
811'.6—dc22
                                        2009005895

British Library Cataloguing in Publication data are available.

For Clarke,
WHO LOVES TO LOPE

Acknowledgments

"Arrhythmia," "Blight," "Body : Rhapsody," "Ichthyosaur," "Rhapsody in Grackle," and "Peripatetic" first appeared in *Verse*; "Cruisers" in *Fourteen Hills*; "Lines Composed on an Open Space" in *Columbia Poetry Review*; "Provincetown," "Eyespot," "'Til God Shall Send His Missing Part," and "Ah, Propeller!" in *New Orleans Review*; "Wandering of Light" and "Afield" in DIAGRAM; "Fetus in Orbit" and "Ninety-nine Escaping North Dakota" in *jubilat*; "Cincinnati" in *Sycamore Review*; "Chicago" in *Chicago Review*; "Nativity" in *Boston Review*; "Apotheosis in Bluegrass" and "Test Pilots among the Haymakers" in *Denver Quarterly*; "International Orange" in *Conduit*; "The Pear as a Guitar" and "Drive-by" in *Slope*; "Reliquary" in *Iowa Review*; "Harlem" and "Scarlet" in *Xavier Review*; "Apograph with Lacunae" in *Sonora Review*; "Lines over Seattle" and "Oriflamme in Meadow" in *Bellingham Review*; "Magnolia" and "The Beet as a Bloody Tenet" in *Salt Hill*; "American Adam" in *turnrow*; "The Somnambulist" and "Blunders" in *Field*; "To Walt Whitman in Winter" and "On the Excision of Man" in *Phoebe*; "Song of the Harpooneer" and "Vehicle Disabled" in *Bateau*; "The Persecutors" and "Little Puffer's Phrasebook" in *Notre Dame Review*; "Descent on Walden," "Lines Composed on an Amos Doolittle Print," and "Smithereens" in *Colorado Review*; and "Radiography" in *Five Fingers Review*.

Author Note

The author would also like to acknowledge the following sources:

"Lines Composed on an Open Space" relies on Charles Olson's 1947 monograph *Call Me Ishmael* for its animus.

"Blunders" is an ekphrastic poem based upon Henry de la Beche's 1830 painting *Duria Antiquior*.

"American Adam" harvests language from the journals of Ralph Waldo Emerson, as presented in Robert D. Richardson's biography of Emerson, *The Mind on Fire*, particularly chapter thirty-three, "The Art of Writing. Jacob Boehme."

"Ninety-nine Escaping North Dakota" interprets a line from Jonathan Edwards's journals, found in George M. Marsden's *Jonathan Edwards: A Life*.

"The Somnambulist" is inspired by "The Orchard Keeper," chapter seventy-three of Richardson's *The Mind on Fire*, and also draws upon several lines from Emerson's journals.

Contents

The day wore on, and the sun went down in the west; still the interloper, gloomy and taciturn, made no signs of departing.

—Walt Whitman

INTERLOPER

PROVINCETOWN

The takeoff seems orchid purpureal
We fly this glider over slope
crucifer pilots

What happened to rubber cement—
it glued our chrome
cloudbank f-stop

I harry you as only a harrier can
as hellion
as hedonist

Yokefellow, how steep our swoop
what coastline what distance?

As if we travel well
        as if potentate

The hinge of the engine-less rudder

Solarized
        it sing-songs

SONG OF THE HARPOONEER

The commercial products that cling
like pilot fish

are a subset. Better to fathom

which juggernaut irrupted the Sound
—beluga or humpback

Pike Street injected with flash

but that's no providence. The fish fly
through air

& whosoever catches is bulletproof

Pilots have been pacified
so that very few

remain. But what's at issue? Jets
run upstream & dissolve on cue

Tridents loaded with caviar

To be forked is an honor of sorts
but countless the whales

LINES COMPOSED ON AN OPEN SPACE

There are days when you are lost
when the quarter notes cannot find you
& you wish to take a buffalo down

with an arrow. You play
in the fiddleheads—the hell with Pacific
you're eager for Plains—everything on the surface

but hardly have you settled when it's time for Little Big Horn,
blisters around your mouth, blown clefs

Such is the paleface. He strikes out for frontier
then notation

ICHTHYOSAUR

Under your influence
the Salamander sings

song of my skin
song of my temperature changes

Blue devil lizard
electrify me

Your musical rules for apocalypse
are brilliant

I have conferred
with medulla with ultramarine

You cannot pray
& you weep

only when corrupt

If Christ is a cottonmouth
what color are your gills

where are your teeth?

FETUS IN ORBIT

I played with the pre-cows in outer space

They were cows of a higher mathematics

(amoebas absent hoofs
no tails to sweep the sparkles)

But I was at home in their blacks & whites
the folds, the solar system

Then I was told I would eat a thousand cows

I lay there, disbeliever, like a figure 8 in milk

ARRHYTHMIA

Grace, the aphrodisiac
riddles the bloodstream electric
me sick—no
blessed is the jumpy heart
says Dr. Harvey
heartbeat enthusiast
The man with the lidocaine
defibrillator
& the cold silver
stethoscope pressed to the flesh
hears the skipping chest nut
irregular
the siss-boom skitter beat
my adamant
love
palpitating immaculate
the dirty rush to judgment

TEST PILOTS AMONG THE HAYMAKERS

They glide through the golden piles
A flare of plasma arcs behind them like a wing
They are a metalwork, a plastic recyclable
& haystacks ignite in the stratosphere

It reminds the pilots of a rainstorm in New England
where young men huddled in the honeycomb
smoking cigarettes, copulating, praying

This was before the days of spacesuits—their skin
decided what was tangential. Hexagons in a river
of O_2, the astronauts blink

as if weighed down, as if the thrust of yea-sayers
has bent them prone

TO WALT WHITMAN IN WINTER

Stoked
the pig iron wreck
of what you are

sledge of sleet
the miles the rails the Union
Pacific

Glacier with a cow-
catcher

how many harps
run over

& wit, the conductor?

This must be the engine
that frosts

this the igneous
that rides on lava

this the scream of a revelator
gone deaf in white

CHICAGO

An epicenter in the snow

would not let us make impressions
So I ask you Sandburg to cast a shadow it stutters

like a telegraph with the wires
cut, which if put to lips the sap whirrs

I pee an income stream stocks pork futures

watching the S & P dwindle
The B & O pulls in

to stockyards—steers feeding
on an intermittent feed

Cast your grizzlies into the stream Sandburg
& they will return fourfold

CINCINNATI

Sell by:		03/23/09
Net Wt.	Unit Price	Total Price
1.69	$2.99/lb.	$5.09

Molasses & rum barbecued ribs
The hull of a steamboat

I can picture it anchored in the Ohio
I can see it in the slip

the back of the pig picked clean

I can see the sluice of wastewater
& the river treated

The *Pork* blows its stack

From here, I can descry the fat
running down a washboard

the pickled feet
china plate, the blood in the well

SMITHEREENS

The treetop, at 9.86 meters per second squared
plummets

its canopy a blown parachute

And how will the voluptuous receive dead weight?

Like a windshield

Survivors climb out from the branches
blown as glass

Their speech is vacuum & their tympanum

So we take them in & let them commandeer

In & out of our lives they wander
as hornets

& they will not collect themselves

APOTHEOSIS IN BLUEGRASS

The newborn foals
who will be their talismans?

Tomorrow I bury my Man-of-War
by the mallards & swans

Imagine a stream that gladdens
the bluegrass of God

In the flood
I will float the dead man's float

Yesterday's dogwood limb—a box
of hoof beats. I constellate the a-

symmetry

& this is why I praise the stirrups

BLUNDERS

[1] And Darwin said: let the plesiosaur advance
even as the swordfish saws his neck in two

[2] let sequined reptiles smile
& the whole seafloor
erupt

    [3] Today a metaphor, tomorrow a porpoise

[4] & left hand writes like a fin upon
lagoon

        [5] Heretofore lies
        a doubtful form

[6] & the Lord complained, via the loggerhead,
How then do we prophesy?

AMERICAN ADAM

The godhead climbs up into me
a rocket manufacturer

Blessed are the barren—look to heaven
for stems, what is airborne

My seedcase aluminum

the map of nomenclature
confetti in an updraft of forceps

—

cloudburst. The fluids pool
in footsteps

whooping cranes wear rubbers
on their wingtips

LINES OVER SEATTLE

Here flows the offshore flow

Rainier like a lithograph

Like a false image, sugar in the skim of the latte

float planes taking off for the straits, Space
Needle

We drink port on the roof of a houseboat

drawing pails upward to water the fuchsia

A taste for azure

A silhouette behind the sail

INTERNATIONAL ORANGE

Man encased in stainless

F-16 strafes the inside of the box
loop-the-loops & figure 8's

It's crowded in the planetarium

One can only imagine moonlight immolation

2,000° Fahrenheit

The stick-man, to repeat, is a player

Part of him plays Aces & pick-up sticks
when entranced

Here is his next move:

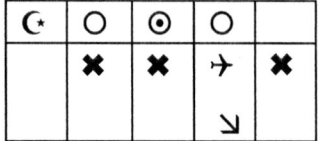

electric oar in the aorta

20,000 feet down, seawater

AH, PROPELLER!

Woe to the seaplane
that wobbles
imperious

lands feet-first
in narrows

The fifth day roils
metallic green

& the skier
harbors in cattails

I saw a man
run out of wetlands
gasoline on his conscience

The malefactor
licked the cut

grasses, hot-sauce

mouth in swale

RADIOGRAPHY

After uranium I eat only winged things
no gills

The Physician orders me to kiss a machine
I'm in love with his scapegoat: the first

to take a bullet in the breastbone
jerks like a wild turkey

After the isotope I drop an enzyme
in plumb & X-ray

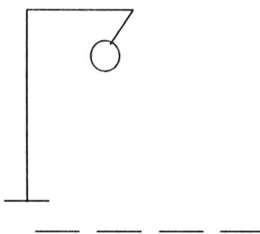

my zones under Pentecost

THE BUTCHER'S MAP

1 *flank*
  it outmaneuvers
the hooks
I have a hunch, look-
ing at feet in a locker
& splitting joint &
gist: feast on white
the apron where Jack-
son Pollock splattered
his rarity

2 *loin*
  or the blue vein is
de-veined; the point
of my cleaver slits
a muscle
marooned between
hemispheres
if a destroyer could
anchor in
groin

3 *chop*
  would the next cut
be any more lean? left
hand on an organ
grinder, hamburger
does beef
believe or do I mean
muse?

4 *rib*
  cartilage seems funda-
mental, I trace the
transition, funny-bones
—& hooves
somewhere kicking up
margin; hence,
cartographer

5 *round*
  of the carcass, I mark
negatives—in my
prime I could stamp
them, now dye
fluorescent the

6 *shank*
  hand with which
I slice the Taurus
& to be truthful
my craft
robotic

7 *neck*
  except at the head
where I salvage
the tongue

SONG OF THE CONSERVATIONIST

The sapsuckers plunder your suet
The lake congeals; once again floe

But the house, gassed, & the giblets
dunked in gravy, & another year swiped

You wish you'd fondled the wattle
as well as neck wrapped in plastic. Yes,

a crime scene, yes, your acreage cordoned

You circle the cul-de-sac with a taste
for spoonbill

LEFT SIDE OF THE LEPIDOPTERIST

If I could capture the Monarch
like a cornflake on a cookie sheet

converse with some other catcher
about lepidoptera—

the Fatal Metalmark

If I could strangle wildflowers in California

& adhere to frontiers
like the Swallowtail

If only the Lost could find the snake-
root

If ever to genuflect again
over lupine & chiasm

If I might sift my quarry
the א of Wright's Metalmark

or trace the razor-cuts of the 88

ORIFLAMME IN MEADOW

Would that the frog camouflaged
no heartbeat no zenith

Instead
the dirty bomb gives up half-life, A♭

Thus cold-blooded
in the palm of your hand, the frolic

—skinned, scored, & measured—
a battlefield of quarter notes

That was yesterday. Today
tadpoles jerk, perpetual eighths

In the mouth of the ibis
the silver chain of a stopwatch

LANDSCAPE WITH CRACK

Little mustang eats thyme

Under a cloudbank
lips crib at the fencepost—mouthfuls of icicles

The eucalyptus by the riverside throw snowballs
chalk dust

Flurries never should have crossed Cascades
& yet stampeded

All things vexed, slapdash

What a wonder the avalanche as it coasts
on serum

& the backhoe bright-eyed with snuff

EIGHTH MAN

Excuse this puncture

while an angstrom of light tumbles
into our theater

See the field, how it opens, compromised
a breastbone

in pieces of ❽?

It's as black as baboon in the cavity—

catacomb for the tumbler

The spiral cuts through all flesh

The wheel of the timing mechanism
revolves like a crocus

In what seems like a garden, rubber hands

A morphine-induced fog supervenes

& EIGHTH MAN sleeps with the wild beasts

& the Ångels wait on him

CRUISERS

The wave runners are tired
adrift in kelp
Men slumped
over handlebars
gunslingers
peering into quiet
derelict as the Portuguese
man-of-war
under their toes
orphic
The friends have scuttled
their tone
& go with tears
sunburnt
   forlornographic
The sailboats have quit
the sun is almandine
& sincere
Only the wedge
of cormorants
rounding the island
only the hyssop
of their wings

BODY : RHAPSODY

      The husk of his car
crumpled like a Coca-Cola
can You stick your head in
the front (passenger) door
& pick through Ovid
& Aristotle covered with
pulverized glass
like sapphires
like sugar
The library is open
& how you remember
your father at a time like this
is excruciating is fire
& smite The world
is aluminum & how you know
is because
        you are the car
& no one (no one else is)
driving

RHAPSODY IN GRACKLE

Like a piano hinge
the scapulars of his wing swing

He titters
a pinecone hemorrhages

The bomb goes dumb
& he can't steer it

nor can caw emancipate the good seed

All he can foresee is sequin
or sentinel

The weeping bombardier woos
his propaganda

The notes he puffs can't sing straight

Another hellfire cone
another iridescence of gray light

THE BEET AS A BLOODY TENET

Though it seems to aspire,
the root is dug out like an Indian Head

& the beet, coiffed, becomes mercantile
—scalp & headdress

The beet
inscribed as a caesarean: all hail winter vegetable!

The beet
on the fingertips of handlers

Last of the heirlooms, it trembles at what the green
grocer did—his ten digits

THE PEAR AS A GUITAR

When the pear is planed
so as to remove toughness, & the stem unstrung

your hand swings over hollow; unlike cello
this instrument is picked. Fingertips

run into the pear & pull out a teardrop

the roar of the pear
as it disappears

MAGNOLIA

[1]Bury the magic marker.

[2]Said pi to the radius,
"I stand alone. Above me,

[3]a wheel of snow. The pig-
ment frozen in water." Reflect
on Heisenberg (h =

[4]Planck's constant). Said the
radius, duplicitous

[5]"Lick magenta
& my pistils."

[6]"I feel sensation, an uncial,"
said π. "I'm apoplectic." Bathe
the root in granulated sugar.

[7]Turn the plant clockwise ½
turn. This will be a hermeneutic.

[8]"4 x π," said r. Do not press

[9]down on seedling, which will
result in nerve damage—destroy-
ing the sheath.

[10]Said π, "Why am I constant-
ly tired? used?" Do not force

[11]the h. Rely on muscle memory

[12]to secure root. Said r, "I
open my mouth & wonderful
things fall out."

WANDERING OF LIGHT

You graze me, purple star
sad blood sack
You dead-end

Nebula

I plastic-bag-pinch
& drop you in a can
oblate

Look up at heedless
the headlights half-decimate

moon, Jupiter

I was sad when the Hyphen
said unto me
go up into the House

of the Interpreter

DRIVE-BY

The tips of the leaves tipsy contusions
I flash my sidearm out the window

at livestock

the redhead I shoot with a .35
& skirt

the marbled, sugar map of the maple

Where to divide these loins
this bottomland green space?

Katydid, possum, longhorn,
berm

& helicopter seeds

pester my liver, ignition

So I come to Part II where I
hyphenate

this U.S. happiness

FUGITIVE MOVEMENTS OF THE POSTLAPSARIANS

Skydivers, they perseverate about heaven

They hang in treetops

& under these canopies they quiver
high-pitched

as if oxygen-deprived

The uplifted, at long last, abandon their silks
& slip post-haste

out of the hangar

True or false, they drink
their beers

& are spirited into Saturns?

Yes or no, they orbit the parking lot
& ejaculate

over the obdurate earth?

HARLEM

Karats karats tumbling to the street

You go back on your hands & knees
& comb the blacktop for glitter

You rake black sands & the smoked
glass of beer bottles
you're in a sluice

What if rock shot through a wind-
shield? What if it punctured an oil pan
Iris?

I am sad to say the aperture
is in your belly—you are a mine-
field

of ice. Your arteries weighted with
ice

The little blue head of your baby
crowns. I take him with forceps

& play his circumference with a stylus

BLIGHT

J. Jesus C. lay your felonious hands on me
Leprosy loves a white-walled skin
Tread's worn, so am I, so's the factory stud
Lift high thou vulcanized rubber tree in the
jungle. Limp snake grip the rim
O pressure

Chrissake robber neighbor
I got nothing but bread in the sack
see?
Seventy-seven slices
Hold me up with your
pistol piece

Kiss my lips wino
        sing me a milk song (suburban, subsistent)

Save your mustard for me

THE REFORMATORY

Tulips under a landfill

They root & toot; they swing a dead cat

To a hothouse where jailed
the lipsticks come up
with blueprints

Add another ninety days for chromatism

In the cooler, pistils

as far as sanguine, ply their trade-
mark

They know a secret, which is how they rocket

CODA:

The tulip always fumed

Whatsoever flammable looses the bulb

It died & was buried fifty feet from atonement

It rose like a sniper & took aim

THE YAM AS RING-NECKED PHEASANT

The oily skin darkens at the throat; the breast
bursts morosely

Carotene bubbles from an exit wound

Insides are raked with the tines of a fork
& flooded with marshmallow foam

Sugar & salt shine—iridescence on the ruffs

I wait again for the cluck-cluck
& swing my sights toward overwrought wings

LINES COMPOSED ON AN AMOS DOOLITTLE PRINT

Against confluence the minutemen misfired

They etched their mess with bayonets

The hawthorn tree reached into a beehive, the pollen
in paper

Whatever wit burst onto green

first revolved in flintlock & flash pan

Then a scarlet letter
                    the wide world in letter-box

Balls of scorch picked off red men

Bees became shuttlecocks, supersonic, as fleeting
as Concord

SIREN IN MIDDLE AGE

You resist this music
which is no music

You've heard it all before on the oboe

& you're sick & tired
of the tinny note

that ice-picks the heart
like a ♮

or a ♭ in the spare tire you've forgotten you carry
wherever you go

When air leaks out
& your tongue wheezes

you tell yourself not to worry not to give it no

lip. Yet still you chase
the pitch

into a dark wood; would that it would decompose

SCARLET

All afternoon the scissor-grinder
pedaled a stone

under the elm
& his wheel sharpened the mother-tongue

filings flying

the ♮s & ♭s
suspended by animal magnetism

& gathered up in bushels
the pittance of the dazzle

THE LIQUID ASTRONOMER

             The stars—
itty-bitty asterisks—
fit neatly inside a tin of snuff

The task they propose
is to displace space

Had they been steamboats
there would have been rivers
& snags

They lack smokestacks anyway

Really what is required is size compressed;
Hence the necessity of a compressor
                        If steamboats

then also turbines, water wheels
sending volumes over gauges edges

Suffice to position stars

MONOPOLY

Power (w/out elocution)
just a token on Baltic

roadster at GO

So the zygote; thereafter, cumulus

It advanced one Christmas
like purple

amassing stars & utilities on exhaust

It was the only hoarfrost for millennia

But then snowman
begat now, №, NW

& he falls, singing, a jingle

I SWALLOWED A DECK OF CARDS

As if a 75 lb. fan off a cotton gin
had been tied to the neck with barbed wire

& the body swamped in the Yazoo

King of Clubs killed King of Spades
one's black; one's more black

When James Byrd was dragged behind a pickup truck
he was a spade; a spade's a spade

I dreamed about a prehistoric bird
Self-propelled, it flew from sea to sea like a bi-plane

That was a wild American Playing Card:

the acrobatic Spade
& the King of Clubs with his ermine spots

'TIL GOD SHALL SEND HIS MISSING PART

Sputter home to a throne room
a diesel seraph
a diesel seraph

The burning helicopter
belly-flops

at rest in suburb

Uplift the engine block & put it in a thorax
& put it in abyss

Coax the maple seed
instruct the carcass

What can be salvaged?

Three sassafras fingers singed
Two spark plugs

One ripcord for the multitude

RELIQUARY

Warehouse full of {angels}

■

rows & rows
of mantises boxed ☐

where is the ■ ? Forklift the wing-

beats

when do these canned meats expire?

I broke the seal
on ceiling ☐

& rolled up {the tin} with a key:
monkeys
in oil

I said: when did these meats expire?

Hallelujah! hands
          rubbing the ■

Let me {in}

🐟		〜	
	✠		👤〜

This electric truck will take you to {text}

Get in the ☐ of the halftrack

                    O

years & years

why half-life? have to?

APOGRAPH WITH LACUNAE

The day tinfoil leaves blew down
we ran electricity out to the garage

That was the day of Daylight
Savings

We gathered a dozen or so black-
birds that had crashed

—lake effect—

& there was room for π
because of the puddles we had run in

The square dance hoe down
whatever

lay with protractor on the draft table

I recall an almanac of circuitry in a box
in the basement

(which we had confused with treasure)

& into the flaw here came
the backhoe

AFIELD

Something old to fondle, Osage
fruits under the stooping

branches—my brother & I threw 'em
I-275
eastbound oranges, sky chopper traffic

Semis kicked hedge-apples interstate
into fences where the sycamores

slough their skins, the retro-
grade bluegrass
stored in Mason jars

& the milky planets
Lucky Charms

Such green children
sweet corn blistering, reentry

LITTLE PUFFER'S PHRASE BOOK

The moon stabbed my throat alas a victim
as if soda can

hissed; the garter at my feet
a black rivulet

of B-flat
The tracheotomy performed

in grass;
wrist

tethered to the ☧

I was dragged to Sound in a bier
as bark peeled from madronas

& sirens patrolled

the inlet;
I left

a half dollar of bliss
for egress

EYESPOT

Aerosol, soot, & emissions
over the archipelago
of my yard

Tigers, Blacks, Giants
aflutter. Aberrant

wings & pollen
pollution yields 33% more

brownout. What I wouldn't
give for an Eighty-Eight
or a Waiter, Comma,

Question Mark

or some such hurricane

THE OMINOUS CROSS

There it goes with the Navigator, the holy rood
dragged out of the Main

& slanted like an Anchor

Thereafter the Crazy Eights drift in open water
for without red flags

no ironclad rules for keeping in place

the 8s are somewhat loopy

more likely to go with the flow than knot; yet
lacking anchorage soon they flag

succumbing to Indefinite. Infinite

the seas where the Eights might wander. Around
& around they go, throwing out

Questions on which to rest

FIGMENT FOR HARP

The harp tilts
The harpist tilts

In the frame
a woody grapevine
a blood red bud

as if she weaves with amputated thumb

The harp rocks in a narrow space
Unlike sex, a to & fro

Yea, even there along the strings
the harp as loom

The harp as electric fence
& on the wires hangs a golden finger

And to think it plays in tune with a cactus

ASIDES TO MY SURGEON

Tattooed arrow on my chest
a line of stitches to unzip

I felt you feeling around in my heart
& so what if it's thick?

So what if it's old growth & a river
bends through it?

Where is the canoe, you asked, the birch bark
& smoke?

You reached for the whole tar nation
the wigwam, the peace pipe

I gave only a hint of direction. It was faint
Even so, you said, I smell blood

TRIPARTITE

termite in a Ziploc   Swabs investigate acid   The mediating thorax—
                           in the digestive tract

he bag sweats   what but a fold-out map
if a President has been shot   that brought the House down   where the inquest flexes

he barely breathes   & the film that sits on a slide   over the Constitution?
                            because it forecast

THE PEAR AS A CRISIS

With a serrated blade I halve the fruit
    & scoop out the stem

    The cut smells like smoke

& gruyére, in fact, fruit flies hover over the crater, O

what did I remove from flesh—a microphone
into which is mouthed

    The knife is going down, the planet

in sum? There's an emergency; the patient
asks for a straw to poke into her throat & we

take turns breathing
whispering through plastic as I drink from her plane

As flies plunge
into Plains, the pear is slipping off the runway

    How do I go on stabbing her oval?

WHAT I SURMISE OF APOCALYPSE

As a wasp grounded in snow
divines sunlight

(or speckled breast)

there I go abrading my feelers—iced

The tongue can't be angered. It licks
like friction

until formaldehyde, an organ
of dirge

a dirigible of prowess

How long ago the thrasher

apostrophized
between fluid & flammable

eclipsed
& spooned the song into her young

Time, times, half a time

THE RAINMAKER

Who wants these radishes from Mars?

Maybe the government which loves to quarantine
& impose tariffs

A kingdom for said contraband if only to bury the red planets
in the desert

Lest they improve, half-life by half-life, into pomegranates

Ah the buzz they will engender if dispersed

Render the meltdown unto Presidents; I will still sublimate
with my dirty fruit

Call it hubbub; call it interference

NOTES TO YOURSELF ON YOUR 40ᵀᴴ

You gape at the Milky Way
Open wide the telescope
eyepiece in socket

Surrender to the galaxy
orbit obit
specs

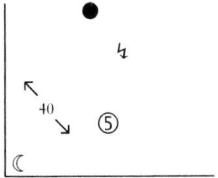

Your child drafting his own star map
arrives as a Jupiter consecrated

THE LEEK AS BAZOOKA

Or elephant gun
aimed by a man in a pith helmet

& thereafter gray matter crumples
in East Africa

Or North
where pyramids

triangulate along the Nile
& signal satellites

I forget
where this is going

admits the man in the pith
helmet, absentmindedly

pitching his saggy tent
in the graveyard

of the leek. The leek that was once
supple & hairy

The leek that undermined peace
in the mouth of the Delta

NEBUCHADNEZZAR & THE PAPARAZZI

Out of my head, I was grazing like the ox

The street was planted with stargazers

& in full bloom were the microphones

of the Press

My name was smeared after the cigar butt

of the sun had fizzled out West

& my hands had left hoof prints on wet cement

Via satellite, hips wobbled on the big screen

& my tail swished. I wished I had been branded

instead of catapulted into Times

Square. I followed the glitz & my own star

into a city of manholes

ON A STICK OF BUTTER IN JULY

The planes bowed & the edges
rounded

the hexahedron slides
across the plate
an iceberg that has calved

A horsefly fouls in the strait

No one lifts a finger. No one
knifes the gilded pest

This all began in a grassy vale
in a cow's mouth, the sweet cud
& the udder

How quickly we arrive at stable

The fly, on manure, beatified
the cow hallowed

& the milking machine
stainless

We barely recall the tipping point

ON THE EXCISION OF MAN

Into the mangrove the propeller stalled

& the petered-out momentum
carved
as if it followed a hyphenated line

magic-marked on a manatee
spiral blade gutting
until the contents (under pressure)
escaped like a can of Alphabet

Soup & the skin shredded, felt like
a man-of-war

You could repeat this Act / trap door into histrionics

inasmuch to say the water evermore emerald
(the whirl ubiquitous)

ON THE EXCISION OF C FROM AD

The comedian upstaged us

We laughed when she told the truth
how she tap-danced across the tiles
Like a chess piece
Queen had lost King

There is a controversy about magi
in these parts—
first of all, wisdom
wisecracker
wizened

Then she put her hand to our hearts
& we dwarfed

which is why (applause)

the Bishop sat down
to drink from her saucer of tears

THE NUMBERS

All my days in a spaceship
the refrigerator box upright

cardboard & barcodes

Suddenly I discover the skew
rhombus

I streak past on a spreadsheet

What I sketch as a magic upset
blurs

or, as others suggest, splashes

True I space-walk in the attic
there are boxcars & a locomotive

but no train tracks

If I bleed the dollhouse
how many G's?

CHARGERS ⚡

As by convection
rubber bubbled on asphalt

as by injection
fuel quickened the Formula 1s

Jumper cables $\dfrac{red}{black}$ colluded & sparked

what of the $\dfrac{\oplus}{-}$ survived electrocution?

In a pacemaker the ♀ received the ♂ & thus
on this cloverleaf

Eights circumscribed the ovals

Seventy-times-seven they blew through
the circuit

VEHICLE DISABLED

The winch of the tow truck pulled
me up by the scruff
my GPS down & I listened to the road
the rumble the insane traffic

I had no more use for a steering wheel
than an ❽ ball or a compass in fluid
on the dash—
uplifted, my crankshaft my wrists my side

Give me a crucifix & a Star
that I might plot my direction & stand up
Rocket of the Apocalypse

ISLAND OF THE INTEGERS

11 collapsed into the crater
who sinned who made the world uneven?

I received the news, a javelin in the slipstream

Foxes & peacocks forsook cages & puffed

⑨muses ⑨ virgins ⑨ months

How did Armageddon begin? Jets-Giants?

Men smelled my hymen—I wandered lonely as a 1

NINETY-NINE ESCAPING NORTH DAKOTA

When day fails, search by flashlight:
don't let the lambs get into the field & wrong the crop

The sheep in eclipse, the wool in shadow

Goodbye to them as they complain

You pinch the edges of a tablet—your sleeping pill
feels like chastisement

(because you cannot swallow)

Night, where one becomes one hundred
& rain fills the craters

& the herd fords the flood

Goodbye to them as they complain

The flock in cataract, the indistinct fighting for sun-
flowers

(*Behold the Lambs!*)

With your crook, you immerse the wayward
& the Badlands drink them in

APOCRYPHAL ANIMALS OF THE BIBLE

Israel & Palestine hector my hippocampus

Gray matter & white matter
riding a seahorse

The Dead Sea

      & the seizure

Two or more pomegranates skinned by a taxidermist

Sand, landing strip, reeds
& rose of Sharon

      speak the language of F-14

to unicorns stranded in the Garden of Eden

Will you ask the battleship that guards leviathan
the way to antimatter?

      Now Red Sea runs aground on my islet

Did I load the mercy seat in this warhead?

PERIPATETIC

The pine threw down its needles

The squirrel played in a pile

What a strange response
to the loss of tingle

Spine cannot budge—the feet
tucked

Suppose a hunchback that foundered was found
to be a pole, bipolar

Yea, humpback in the flammable sea
yea, pin-cushion with pikes

SONG OF THE GRAY AVIATOR

In trust we approach the sound of true
& frolic in experimental planes

You, for example, flew into a rage
plastic flamingo

To you I drift, a spitfire on cloud nine

Mockingbird I light from tree to tree
Who hasn't been smoked?

Remember me (remember tailspin)
as a carbon copy of paradise

FOWLING-PIECE

After the fly-by, I lay trigger-happy
in my hunting blind & looked skyward
& honked in artificial sympathy

Unless you go invisible & lie similarly, unless
you too shoot birds of a feather

your goose is cooked, I more than once said
with a mouthful of casings

*   *   *   *   *   *

When the fuselages passed over, when
the longnecks descended

you blew your cover & all your ganglia

or stars over camouflage announced a swerve
in strategy

I out of my covert, you out of your gaggle,
all night in antiphon we shot our mouths off
we shot the breeze

DESCENT ON WALDEN

Seven notes to woo an owl
or a chopper

The ice opens in a circle—atomic blast

Even the pond seems inside-out

Standing on rudiments, a vital heat
pierces our heels

The yield of the pencil factory up in smoke

This the day of minutemen

But where his parable is utmost

a loon gleans the edges of a bean field &

the queer iris in the slipknot blooms

SONG OF THE FORESTER

Squirrel you ate my acorns & now I clutch no saplings
The pith
          of the hardwood has been masticated

Is it true that the cellulose in your entrails can be unspooled
like a film strip?

And what if I scan it—will it shade me broad & leafy
will it culminate?

The wild pigs on the hillside will also wonder as they rut

I liken them to hieroglyphs

for they cipher as if sunstruck. This leads to the radical
so familiar among the clear-cut:

          the root & the echo of its freefall

THE NOMENCLATORS

In the garden of philosophy, we tend
our heads

We perseverate about cabbage

We hack at cauliflowers

And our brains contemplate each kink
of the hose

which, like the morning glory,
loops its signature

around every plant fit to eat

The names of our vegetables
are signed in a stranglehold

so that as the tomato turns purple
we know it as Cherokee

Barely has it been plucked before our breath
is shortened

& daylight pinched

It feels like a sentence
all our extravagance in a slipknot

while the hose pumps alphabets of gladness

& the cerebellum prays without ceasing

THE PERSECUTORS

The feathers make a point
like a paintbrush

the bill a spearhead which crucifies fish

& so the bird, in all directions, a pointillist

What you wouldn't predict is a cougar
to eat every one of those bones

& so Audubon devoured the Sandhill Crane

which is disheartening since he himself
is now bagged & mounted

I will say it again: an artist divided against himself
cannot tranquilize

& so the painter slays the cougar

as if his Head is the object

as if, long-legged, he wades into perspective

THE SOMNAMBULIST

When it happens, you're glad it's not you
but then you wake up hammered

in the lost orchard—woozy
from Bloodgood & Spitzenbergs

& quinces from Persia

As you veer unpiloted through space
you realize the plum is unattainable—

though each germ a jet of flame, your prize
has expired from saturnalia

Elliptic, the slugs on the pear leaves
broil in their own fat

& flickers drill asterisks into cherry

Yes, you say, lead me to the happy violence
by which I am imparadised

NATIVITY

Now I lay my iceberg to sleep

his $\frac{7}{8}$ kicking at comforter

Sebastian, he endures icicles

that perforate what his life should be.
The newborn

for I have calved him

& what of St. who lies under the 98°
of me?

I did not make him up—I summoned the ice-
maker

& he delivered exclamations